For the Love of Sophia
Wisdom Stories
from Around the World
and Across the Ages

David W. Jones

Valjean Press, Nashville

David Jones is pastor of
Harpeth Presbyterian Church,
Brentwood, Tennessee
and is also the author of:

The Psychology of Jesus:
Practical Help for Living in Relationship

In the Beginning Were the Words:
A Look at the First Chapters of
Genesis through Poetry

The Enlightenment of Jesus:
Practical Steps to Life Awake

Moses and Mickey Mouse:
How to Find Holy Ground in the Magic Kingdom
and Other Unusual Places

Enough:
and Other Magic Words to
Transform Your Life

for more information, see:
www.davidwjonesbooks.com

And now, my children, listen to me:

    happy are those who keep my ways.

Hear instruction and be wise,

    and do not neglect it.

Happy is the one who listens to me,

    watching daily at my gates,

    waiting beside my doors.

For whoever finds me finds life

    and obtains favor from the Lord;

but those who miss me injure themselves;

    all who hate me love death.

Proverbs 8

Sophia has built her house,

    she has hewn her seven pillars.

She has slaughtered her animals,

    she has mixed her wine,

    she has also set her table.

She has sent out her servant-girls,

She calls from the highest places in the town,

    "You that are simple, turn in here!"

To those without sense she says,

    "Come, eat of my bread

    and drink of the wine I have mixed.

    Lay aside immaturity, and live,

    and walk in the way of insight."

Proverbs 9

Introduction

Dear Reader,

This book is for lovers of wisdom.

These stories, though from many religions, cultures, and eras were all told by wisdom lovers. In their original form, they had vivid central characters like Baal Shem Tov, Mulla Nasruddin, Lao Tzu, Buddha, and others. For this collection, I've rewritten them around a single persona, Sophia.

Sophia is Greek for wisdom.

Socrates, Plato, and other sages described themselves as *philo-sophia,* or *lovers of wisdom.*

In the Septuagint, the Greek translation of the book of Proverbs, *Sophia* is the personification of wisdom (see Proverbs 8 & 9 on the previous pages).

In this book, Sophia serves us as a central character weaving the following stories into a unified whole. Unlike Buddha, Jesus, Rabbi, Master, Monk, Priest, Guru, or even Teacher, Sophia is not bound by history, tradition, or thousands of years of speculation. While those names and titles distract us (most of us haven't heard of Mulla Nasruddin or Baal Shem Tov), binding us in labeling exercises on *who* and *what* they were or are, with Sophia, we can skip over *who* and *what* labeling and focus on the story, the character, not *who* but *how,* not *what she is* but *what she says,* opening our ears and our minds to the messages of the stories.

For these stories, Sophia is, as the Apostle Paul described himself, *all things to all people.* As a character, she is flexible and malleable. She can be young or old, mature or childish, judicious or mischievous, whatever the story needs her to be, whatever you need her to be, to facilitate your insight, vision and understanding.

Sophia also offers another gift, a present too long in coming. Though these stories in their original form vary in style, language, and approach, they all share one common characteristic – the central characters, the wise sages or insightful fools, have always been male. Having collected these stories for the last twenty years, it saddens me how the central characters in these wisdom traditions are almost never women. In my life, contrary to the stories, I have had many wise women who have advised me, many Sophias who have challenged me.

In order to attempt to move the scales slightly to a more balanced perspective, Sophia serves us with an alternative image to the traditionally masculine sages.

For this assortment, I owe a great debt to the work of Anthony de Mello who compiled many of these stories and others in his collections. His work was a great starting point for this anthology. Because my collection comes over several years, any direct copy of a story without credit was unintentional.

Enjoy these stories and may they help you, as Sophia encourages in Proverbs 9, *walk in the way of insight and live!*

David Jones 2010

Contents

☙Wake up❧

"Sophia, what's the opposite of intelligence?" a student asked.

"Ignorance," she replied.

"Then what is the opposite of wisdom?"

"Ignore-ance."

One day, Sophia walked out onto a sidewalk, stood still, and waited. A man, head down, not paying attention, walked right into her.

"I'm sorry," he said.

"Wake up!" she yelled.

"I didn't mean to bump..."

"Wake up!" she yelled again.

He looked at her sternly, "Do I know you?"

"Don't you?" she asked.

"I..."

"Wake up!" she yelled again.

The man walked quickly around her and ran on down the street. Sophia stood in the middle of the sidewalk and waited.

"Sophia, why do you pray?" asked the skeptic. "Do you pray to make the sun come up?"

"No," replied Sophia, "I pray so that when the sun comes up I will be awake to see it."

❖

"Sophia, what is your religious practice?" a student asked.

"I sit, I walk, and I eat," she replied.

"But, Sophia, everyone sits, walks and eats."

"Ahh," she said, "but when I sit, I know I am sitting. When I walk, I know I am walking. And when I eat, I know I am eating."

❖

"Sophia, what are you?" a student asked.

"What do you mean?" she asked.

"Are you Buddhist?"

"No," she answered.

"Are you Jewish?"

"No," she replied.

"Christian?"

"No."

"Muslim?"

"No."

"Hindu?"

"No."

"Then what?" the frustrated student asked.

"I am a mind awake," Sophia replied.

ೞLook໖

Sophia was asked to speak to the students of a local medical school.

"Sophia, what do we need to be better doctors?" the students asked.

"Doctors," Sophia said, "need strong stomachs and strong powers of observation." Then she opened a canister. The putrid smell quickly moved through the classroom. Sophia stuck a finger in the jar, pulled it up, and then licked it. She passed the jar around, encouraging each doctor in training to do the same. Each did, and though many felt nauseous, no one got sick.

"You all have very strong stomachs," she said. "But your powers of observation need some work."

"What do you mean?" they asked. "We did just what you did."

"There is one difference," she replied. "The finger I dipped in the jar was not the finger I licked."

"How can I find enlightenment?" the student asked Sophia.

"You really want to know?" Sophia asked.

"Yes, desperately," the student said.

Sophia looked one way, then the other, and when certain no one was in sight, she leaned close to the student and whispered, "You must learn the secret act."

"What is the secret act?" the student asked whispering.

"This," Sophia said and she closed her eyes then opened them.

A woman approached her husband.
"What's different about me?" she asked.
"New shoes," he replied.
"No."
"New dress."
"No."
"I give up."
"I'm wearing an elephant costume."

A young widower, who loved his five year old son very much, was away on business when bandits burned down his village and took his son away.

When the man returned, he saw the ruins of his town, his home, and was devastated. Scavenging through the ruins near his home, he found the charred remains of a small body he assumed to be his son.

He grieved, held a funeral, and buried the remains.

Daily he went to the graveside, and nightly he cried alone.

Months later, his real son escaped from the bandits and found his way home. He arrived at his father's new cottage at midnight and knocked at the door. The father, still grieving asked, "Who is it?"

The child answered, "It is me papa, open the door!"

But, convinced his son was dead, the father shouted, "Go away" and continued to cry.

After some time, the child left.

Father and son never saw each other again.

There once was a man who lost his axe. He searched around his yard for the lost axe.

He saw his neighbor's son out playing in the yard next to his. The man watched the boy and, to him, the way the boy walked, his manner of speaking, even the expression on his face seemed to indicate the boy's guilt. The man was convinced beyond a shadow of a doubt that he had discovered what must have happened to his axe.

On the way to confront the boy's father of the crime of the stolen axe, he happened to see the axe leaning against his fence by his gate, right where he left it.

Looking again at his neighbor's son, he noticed how innocent the boy seemed. There was nothing at all in the boy's behavior or appearance that suggested to the man that he had been a thief.

❖

A man encountered Sophia at the market selling used books. As he searched through a pile, Sophia reached below the table, pulled out an old book with a ratty cover, and when certain no one was watching, whispered, "Try this one. It is a treasure."

The man bought it for a few pennies, took it home, read it, and to his surprise, on the inside back cover he found scribbled in tiny letters a few sentences, a brief description, about a magic stone that could turn anything it touched into pure gold. According to the book, the stone was lying somewhere on the shore of the Black Sea among a million other pebbles that looked just like it. The one difference was that the magic stone was warm to the touch whereas all others were cold.

The man set up a tent on the shore and went to work. Each stone he picked up, if it was cold to the touch, he threw it far into the sea so that he wouldn't keep picking up the same stones.

Stone after stone, he picked each up, felt it, and hurled it deep into the water. Stone after stone...

He worked a week, a month, ten months, a whole year, patiently feeling each stone and tossing it into the sea.

Then, one evening, he picked up a pebble, and it was warm to the touch! Through sheer force of habit, he threw it far out into the water.

"Where shall I look for enlightenment?" the student asked Sophia.

"Here," she replied.

"When will it happen?"

"It is happening right now."

"Then why don't I experience it?"

"Because you do not look."

"What should I look for?"

"Nothing, just look."

"At what?"

"Anything your eyes alight upon."

"Must I look in a special kind of way?"

"No. The ordinary way will do."

"But don't I always look the ordinary way?"

" No."

"Why ever not?"

"Because to look you must be here. You're mostly somewhere else."

Sophia was sitting quietly by a stream, enjoying the sound of the brook, when a traveler came up and stood above her and without introduction said, "I've come a long way for a wisdom teaching to guide me through life."

Sophia just stared up at him and said nothing.

Thinking Sophia might be deaf, the man spoke slowly and loudly, "I was hoping you would tell me something that could help me live my life to its fullest,"

Sophia stared up at him and then looked to the stream.

"Please, some simple, wise word that could help me," he begged, almost screaming.

"Look," she whispered.

The visitor was perplexed. "Look?" he said. "That's it? Look? That's too brief. I came a long way. I was hoping for something more than just *look*."

"Look," Sophia said emphatically.

He was obviously disappointed.

"Look, look, look!" Sophia said again standing up.

"I don't know what you mean," the stranger said.

Sophia replied, "Look means look!" and with that, she shoved him into the stream.

The discussion among the disciples once centered on the usefulness of reading. Some thought it was a waste of time, others disagreed. When Sophia was asked, she said, "Have you ever read one of those texts in which the notes scrawled in the margin by a reader proved to be as illuminating as the text itself?"

The students nodded in agreement.

"Life," said Sophia, "is one such text."

A traveler asked Sophia how to distinguish a true teacher from a false one when he got back to his own land.

Sophia replied, "A good teacher offers practice; a bad one offers theories."

"But how shall I know good practice from bad?"

"In the same way that the farmer knows good cultivation from bad," she said.

◖See◗

"When will I be enlightened?" the student asked Sophia.

"When you see," Sophia said

"See what?"

"Trees and flowers and moon and stars."

"But I see these every day."

"No. What you see is paper trees, paper flowers, paper moons and paper stars. For you live not in reality but in your words and thoughts. For you to truly see, you don't need new landscapes. You need new eyes."

"What does Sophia teach?" asked a visitor.

"Nothing," said the students.

"Then why does she give sermons and lessons?"

"She only points the way – she teaches nothing. If Sophia were to teach, we would make beliefs out of her teachings. She is not concerned with what we believe - only with what we see."

"Of what use is Sophia?" someone asked.

"To show you what you have always known, to show you what you are always looking at," the student replied.

When this confused the visitor, the student exclaimed, "An artist, by his paintings, taught me to see the sunset. Sophia, by her lessons, shows me to see the reality of every moment."

❖

Sophia was passing through town and needed a place to stay. Though many from the congregation she visited, including the pastor, offered her a place to sleep, she asked permission to stay in the church.

The next morning, the members of the congregation came to the church to visit Sophia but found she was gone and their church had been vandalized. Someone had painted, *Beware! Beware! Beware!* all over the church – including the sanctuary. *Beware!* on the pulpit. *Beware!* on the choir loft. *Beware!* on the front door going out.

They were angry at first and started to clean the words off their beloved church, but they realized that Sophia must have painted the words on their building. They wondered together.

"*Beware?* Is she encouraging us to be afraid? Is there a terrible tragedy or calamity coming?" one asked.

"Sophia, like the Bible, encourages us not to be afraid. I don't think she's encouraging us to be anxious," another added.

"She is often encouraging us to be awake, to be aware... to beware. Sophia painted these words around us to encourage us to be awake, to be aware," another member added.

"*Beware* is written on the pulpit. We should beware of the Bible." From that day forward, they were. They looked to the Bible for a word from God, but were wary to never use it to beat others with their beliefs.

"*Beware* is on the choir loft. We should beware of our prayers." From that day forward, they were wary of their prayers and took not just their own needs but other's as well to God.

"*Beware* is written on the door. We should be wary of how we go into the world." From then on, they went out into their community and beyond and sought to live their faith for the benefit of others.

A group of students came upon Sophia outside her home. She was looking through the bushes and in the grass of her yard. "What are you looking for?" the students asked.

"Oh," she said seeming surprised to see them. "I am looking for the key to my house."

"We will help you," her students replied.

After about an hour of searching, a student asked, "Where did you lose your key?"

Sophia pointed to her home, "Inside my house."

All the students looked up at Sophia and asked, "Then why are you looking out here?"

"The light is better out here," she laughed and walked back inside her house.

Later she told them, "Enlightenment only comes when we shine light in our dark places."

There once was a man who had two great fears, shadows and footsteps. One day, he looked over his shoulder to see his shadow. Frightened, he started running. As he ran, he heard footsteps and became more afraid. The faster he ran the more footsteps he heard. He finally died of exhaustion.

❖

We understand why children are afraid of darkness, but why are adults afraid of light?

Plato

Once, a monk, while praying in his room, saw a large spider descending in front of him. Each day, as he began to pray, the spider would descend and he would run away. After several days of interrupted prayer, he went to the kitchen and returned with a butcher knife. On the way back to his room, he saw Sophia in the hallway.

"Where are you going?" Sophia asked.

"I'm going back to my room to pray," he said.

"How are you going to pray with a knife?" Sophia asked.

"Everyday, as I begin my prayers, a spider drops from the ceiling and interrupts me. Today, I'm going to kill the giant spider with this knife."

"Fine," said Sophia. "Before you stab the spider, get some paint and mark it with an X."

The student did as Sophia instructed. He started to pray, the large spider descended in front of him. He painted it with an X. As soon as he painted the X, the spider disappeared.

Puzzled, he got up and walked around his room. He looked in the mirror to see a large X painted on his head.

❖

In a convent, a nun was accused of sneaking in men.

When the leaders stormed into her room, they found her sitting on a barrel.

Sophia knew there was a man in the barrel, but waited until all the other sisters left, then whispered to the accused, "Sister, be on guard. Pay attention to yourself."

Then Sophia left the room.

To a student who was worried constantly, Sophia said, "Give me your mind, and I will put it at rest."

The student thought long and hard on how to respond, then said, "When I look for it, I can't find it." Then he worried no more.

❖

Just as darkness is an absence of light, so evil is an absence of awareness. What do you do with an absence?

Anthony de Mello

❖

Sophia told her students, "People often choose to hold onto jealousies and anxieties, resentments and guilt, because these negative emotions provide them with the feeling of being alive."

"Why would people choose such negative thoughts?" asked a student.

Sophia then told this story, "The local postman took a shortcut through a meadow on his bicycle. Midway across, a bull spied him and gave chase. The poor fellow barely made it to the fence.

"A neighbor who watched him run asked, 'That bull nearly got you, didn't he?'

"The postman replied, 'Yes, nearly gets me every time.'"

"How shall I rid myself of fear?" the student asked.

"How can you rid yourself of what you cling to?" Sophia responded.

"You mean I actually cling to my fears? I cannot agree to that."

"Consider what your fear protects you from, and you will see your folly."

Sophia saw an old friend. "What were you doing at the church today?" she asked.

The friend replied, "I went to confession."

Sophia asked, "You went to confession? I can't imagine you committing a grave sin. What did you confess?"

"I confessed I was too lazy to go to Mass, that I yelled at a gardener, and that I drove my Mother out of the house."

"Yes, but that was all years ago. Surely you've been to confession since then."

"Yes, I have. But I confess it every time. I like to remember it."

He who lives in harmony with himself lives in harmony with the universe.

Marcus Aurelius

An active young woman showed signs of stress and strain. The doctor prescribed tranquilizers and asked her to report to him after a couple of weeks.

When she came back he asked her if she felt any different. She said, "No, I don't. But I've observed that others seem a lot more relaxed."

"I meant for you to take the medicine," the doctor said. "Not give it to your family and friends."

"Here," said Sophia, "take this lamp."

"I don't need a lamp," said the man. "I am blind."

"It is not for you to see with but for others to see you," Sophia told him.

While walking across a bridge at night, another man bumped into him. "What's the matter?" said the blind man. "Can't you see the lamp?"

"No," said the man. "Your candle is not lit."

❖

A distressed person came to Sophia for help. She asked, "Do you really want a cure?"

"If I did not, would I bother to come to you?" he responded.

"Oh, yes," she said. "Most people do."

"What for?"

"Not for a cure," she said. "Cures are too painful. They

simply want relief. Only when you are willing to endure the discomfort of truly seeing yourself can you find health."

A distraught man approached Sophia. "Please, Teacher, I feel lost, desperate. I don't know who I am. Please, show me my true self!"

Sophia just looked away without responding.

The man began to plead and beg, "Please, show me who I am. I want to know."

When Sophia did not reply, the man gave up and started to leave. At that moment, Sophia called out to him by name.

"Yes?" the man said as he spun back around.

"There it is!" she exclaimed.

Sophia sat down next to a woman on a bench who was crying. "Why are you crying?" Sophia asked.

"Because everyone is happy, except me," she moaned. She turned to Sophia, "Why am I not happy like other people?"

"Because they have learned to see goodness and beauty everywhere, and you haven't," Sophia replied.

"Why don't I see goodness and beauty everywhere?"

"Because you cannot see outside of you what you fail to see inside. You are like the beggar who sat on the street every day with a bowl begging for pennies. She never noticed the bowl she was using to beg, but if she had, she would have seen it was an ancient bowl with wonderful designs. If she had taken the bowl to be appraised, she would have discovered it was a priceless treasure."

"What does the bowl symbolize?" the student asked.

"You," Sophia replied. "You beg everyday for penny affirmations, when your life would be so much richer if you would only see the treasure you are!"

❖

Sophia was sitting with a group of children, "What do you want to be when you grow up?" she asked.

"A doctor," said one. "A teacher," said another. Each shared their dreams for the future, all except one little child.

"What about you?" Sophia asked. "What do you want to be?"

"I want to be possible," was the reply.

"Possible, what do you mean?" asked Sophia.

"Everyone says to me, 'You are impossible.' So, when I grow up, I want to be possible."

"So shall you be," said Sophia.

❦ Live ❧

Sophia asked her students, "Which of you knows the fragrance of a rose?"

All of them indicated that they knew.

Then she said, "Put it into words."

All of them were silent.

"Tell me about apples," said Sophia to her students.

The first student, in the length of a lecture, explained the origin of apples and how apples were introduced into their culture.

The second student drew a graph and pointed out the marketing uses for apples in cider, desserts, and applesauce.

The third said nothing. Instead he took out a pen knife, cut a wedge, slipped it into Sophia's mouth and gently pushed her jaw upward so that the apple would squish inside her mouth.

"Precisely," said Sophia. "Apples cannot be explained with words. They must be experienced on the tongue. The only way to know about apples is with your mouth shut."

Sophia added, "After all, the word *sun* can't make you warm. The word *water* can't clean you. And the word *bread* can't make you full."

❖

"Who knows what time is?" Sophia asked her class.

"What time it is?" a student asked.

"No," replied Sophia. "What time is."

The class thought for a moment and several students raised their hands, but when she called on each one, none had an answer.

❖

"What is it you seek?" asked Sophia of a scholar who came to her for guidance.

"Life," he replied.

"Life can only be found by looking beyond your words, thoughts, and images."

"What do you mean?" the scholar asked.

"You are constantly searching but not finding because you are trying to live in a world of ideas, a world of words. You try and feed on words, but you are hungry for life. A menu will not satisfy your hunger. A formula will not satisfy your thirst."

❖

"I have traveled a great distance to listen to Sophia, but I find her words quite ordinary," said a traveler.

"Don't listen to her words," the student advised. "Listen to her message."

"How does one do that?"

"Take hold of a sentence that she says. Shake it well until all the words drop off. What is left will set your heart on fire."

❖

A suitor wrote letters upon letters to his beloved while away. When he finally returned, he said to her, "See, I wrote you all these letters of love while we were apart." He pulled them out and began to read them to her.

"Foolish boy," she said. "These letters are all about your longing for me. I'm sitting here in front of you and you are lost in your words!" Then she kissed him, and he awoke.

❖

In the depth of my soul there is a wordless song.
Kahlil Gibran

"What are you afraid of?" Sophia asked.
"The future. I have no idea of what tomorrow will bring."
Sophia laughed, "You are afraid of tomorrow, not realizing that yesterday is just as dangerous."

❖

"How can I have fuller life?" asked the student.
"Come into the present moment," replied Sophia.
"Am I not in the present moment?" asked the student.
"No, you are still trying to live in the past."
"Why should I drop my past? Not all of it is bad."

"You don't drop the past because it is bad or good," replied Sophia. "You drop the past because it is dead, gone, not real, mere images in your mind. You can't live in images."

Don't let yesterday use up too much of today.

Will Rogers

❖

A student asked Sophia about her lessons, "Why do you not teach repentance."

"I do teach repentance," she replied. "The difference is when I teach repentance, I don't talk about sorrow for the past. The past is dead and not worth a moment's grief. Repentance is not own your mistakes and take your punishment, but instead, repentance is own your mistakes and let them go. Yesterday is gone. No matter how hard you try or guilty you feel you cannot live in yesterday. Today is all you have."

❖

A dispute took place between her students. Sophia called them together and said, "To be wronged is nothing unless you insist on remembering it. For example, a burglar found this sign on the door of a safe he was about to blow, 'Please do not use dynamite. This safe is not locked. Just turn the knob.' The instant he turned the knob a sand bag fell on him and a siren woke the neighborhood. When a friend visited the man in prison he found him bitter, 'How am I ever going to trust another human being again?' he asked."

Then Sophia added, "So often, we only live the past and close our minds to the present. Just because you were hurt in the past, doesn't mean you'll be hurt today. Choose love. Choose hope. Choose faith. Live today."

❖

After ten years of marriage, the wife made her husband promise that if she died, he would not marry another. "If you see another woman after I die," she said, "I will haunt you."

Ten years later, the woman did die.

After a time, the man started to date. He fell in love and got engaged. Then the ghost of his wife appeared each night and tormented him. Looking for help, he went to Sophia.

"Hmmm," said Sophia. "When she comes again, flatter her, and tell her that she knows much more than you do. Then tell her to answer one question, and if she can answer this one question, you'll break off the engagement."

"Okay," said the man. "What is the question?"

"Take a handful of beans and ask her how many beans you have in your hand. If she can answer it correctly, then you'll know it is the ghost of your wife, if not, you'll know that she is an image in your mind, an attachment you have of your past."

That night, the ghost appeared, "You know a lot more than I," he told her.

"I know you went to see Sophia today," she said.

"Yes, I did," he said. "If you can answer me one question, I will break off my engagement, but if not, you must go away."

"Deal," she said.

He turned and grabbed a handful of beans. When he turned back, she was gone.

Sophia ferrying a man across a piece of rough water asked, "You from around here?"

"Your question lacks a verb," the man replied. "You should have asked, 'Are you from around here?' Have you never studied grammar?" asked the scholar.

"No," Sophia replied.

"Then half of your life has been wasted."

Sophia paddled on, and then noticed the raft had sprung a leak. She then asked the passenger. "Have you ever learned how to swim?"

"No!" he exclaimed looking at the water filling the raft.

"Well," she said, "I guess your whole life has been wasted."

❖

A man went to see the village counselor. "When I go to bed, I am so afraid there are monsters under my bed that I can't sleep. It is so bad, I even tried sleeping under my bed, but then I was certain there were monsters on top and still couldn't sleep. What can I do?"

"I think I can help you," said the counselor. "Go buy these roots and berries, take them twice a day, and come see me three times a week. In three years, I think I can cure you."

"I have no other choice," the man said, "Sign me up."

But then the man didn't come back, so the counselor went to his home. "I thought you were going to begin treatment."

"I was," the man said, "but now I'm sleeping fine."

"What made the difference?"

"Well, after I talked to you, I went to see Sophia. I told her my problem. She came to my house. Then she cut the legs off my bed."

☙Choose❧

Sophia was sitting in one of her regular places under the shade of an oak tree. She was about to fall asleep, when a group of children approached.

"Teacher," they cried out, "we have gathered all the oranges under a tree and wish to divide them equally among ourselves. There are three of us but we have only twenty oranges. We all worked to gather them and have searched for another but found none. It seems that one of us must be deprived of an orange but we cannot decide which. Will you help us decide?"

Sophia listened carefully to their impassioned plea and thoughtfully asked, "Would you rather I decide this matter with God's justice or human justice?"

The children were puzzled. They asked Sophia to wait while they conferred.

One boy said, "Human judges take bribes. If we say human justice, Sophia might take some of our oranges. God is supposed to be just. I vote for God's justice."

The second agreed, "Human justice is often corrupt."

The third added, "Since Sophia is a holy woman, don't holy women produce miracles. If we pick God's justice, maybe she can produce one more orange."

In agreement they spoke to Sophia, "We choose God's justice."

"You have chosen well," Sophia said with a smile. Then, to the first boy she gave fifteen oranges, to the second four, to the third one.

Then she told them, "God created the oranges. God gave you the power to choose what to do with them."

The boys left Sophia and returned to their village where they found more friends and shared their oranges.

One day a small boy decided to play a trick on Sophia. He took her a grasshopper cupped in his hands. "Sophia, is the grasshopper in my hands alive or dead?" he asked.

Knowing if she said it was alive he would crush it and if she said it was dead he would let it hop away, she replied, "Ah, my young friend, it is whatever you choose."

❖

A beautiful girl in the village was pregnant. Her angry parents demanded to know who the father was. At first resistant to confess, the anxious and embarrassed girl finally pointed to the local rabbi. The outraged parents confronted the rabbi with their daughter's accusation. The rabbi simply replied "Is that so?"

When the child was born, the parents brought it to the rabbi, who now was viewed as a pariah by the whole village. They demanded that he take care of the child since it was his responsibility.

"Is that so?" he replied calmly as he accepted the child.

For many months he took very good care of the child until the daughter could no longer withstand the lie and confessed that the real father was a young man in the village. The parents immediately went to the rabbi to see if he would return the baby. Apologizing, they explained what had happened.

"Is that so?" he said as he handed them the child.

There once was a strict monastery. Following a vow of silence, no one was allowed to speak at all except every ten years, the monks were permitted to say two words. After spending his first ten years at the monastery, one monk went to the head monk. "It has been ten years," said the head monk. "What are the two words you would like to speak?"

"Bed... hard..." said the monk.

"I see," replied the head monk.

Ten years later, the monk returned to the head monk's office. "It has been ten more years," said the head monk. "What are the two words you would like to speak?"

"Food... stinks..." said the monk.

"I see," replied the head monk.

Yet another ten years passed and the monk once again met with the head monk who asked, "What are your two words?"

"I... quit!" said the monk.

"Well, I can see why," replied the head monk, "all you ever do is complain."

Most folks are about as happy as they make up their minds to be.
Abraham Lincoln

Sophia set up a produce stand at a local farmer's market.

Unlike the other stands of fruits and vegetables, Sophia had no produce in front of her stand.

A woman approached, "What do you sell here?"

"What do you want?" Sophia asked.

"What do you mean, 'What do you want?'"

"Just that," Sophia replied. "What do you want? Whatever you want, you can get it here."

The woman laughed at her, "Well then, I want peace of mind, love, and freedom from fear." After thinking for a moment, she added, "Not just for me, but for the whole world."

"Great!" Sophia said. "But you understand, I don't sell the produce, I just sell the seeds. It's your job to go out and help them grow."

Sophia approached a king who was preparing for war.

"O King, if we conquer Rome, what will we do next?"

"Sicily is next door and will be easy to take," he replied.

"And what shall we do after Sicily is taken?" Sophia asked.

"Then we will move over to Africa and conquer Egypt."

"And after Egypt?"

"Then Greece will come."

"And what, may I ask, will be the benefit of all these conquests?"

"Then," said the king, "we can sit down and enjoy ourselves."

"Can we not," asked Sophia, "choose to enjoy ourselves now?"

"How are you today, Sophia?" a man asked.

"I am so fine," she replied.

"Why are you so fine?" he asked.

"Because I choose to be," she replied.

❖

A monkey threw a coconut at Sophia. She opened it, drank the milk, and made a bowl from its shell.

❖

Sophia was sleeping on the pier, her fishing rod by her side.

"Why aren't you fishing," the busy man asked.

"Because I've caught enough for the day," Sophia replied.

"Why don't you catch more?"

"What would I do with them?"

"Sell them."

"What for?"

"So you would have more money."

"Why?"

"So you could buy a boat, catch more fish, make more money."

"What would I do then?" Sophia asked.

"Then you could enjoy yourself," the man replied.

"What do you think I am doing now?" she asked.

❖

"Nothing is good or bad, but it's all in how you think about it," Sophia said to her students.

When asked to explain, she said, "A person cheerfully observed a religious fast seven days a week. Her neighbor starved to death on the same diet."

❖

A man who took great pride in his lawn found himself with a large crop of dandelions. He tried every method he knew to get rid of them. Still they plagued him. Sophia came upon him in his yard, on his hands and knees, pulling them out one by one, complaining over each one. Sophia laughed and said, "You might be happier if you would choose to love them."

❖

To a woman who was depressed every day, Sophia gave a coin. "With this coin," Sophia told her, "you will be able to see what kind of day destiny has in store for you. Flip it every morning. If it comes up heads, you are about to have a great day.

After a week of great days, the woman looked at the coin. It had heads on both sides.

❖

Sophia and a student came upon a blind man sitting on the sidewalk, begging.

Sophia said, "Give the man some money."

The student dropped ten dollars in the beggar's hat.

Sophia said, "You should have tipped your hat as a mark of respect."

"Why?" asked the student.

"One always should show respect when giving money."

"But the man was blind," the student protested.

"You never know," said Sophia, "he may be faking."

Happiness does not depend on outward things, but on the way we choose to see them.

Leo Tolstoy

❖

Sophia and a student were washing their bowls in the river when they noticed a scorpion that was drowning. Sophia scooped it up and set it upon the bank. In the process she was stung. She went back to washing her bowl and again the scorpion fell in. Sophia saved the scorpion and was again stung. The student asked her, "Sophia, why do you continue to save the scorpion when you know its nature is to sting?"

"Because," Sophia replied, "to save it is my nature."

❖

The village was terrified of a coming army of Samurai. Everyone hid in their homes except Sophia who went out to meet the army on the bridge to the village.

The army arrived on their horses and found Sophia standing on the bridge. The head Samurai dismounted and walked to the bridge, "Lady," he said drawing his sword, "don't you know I am someone who can kill you in an instant?"

"Sir," she replied, "don't you know I am someone who can die in an instant?"

The Samurai mounted his horse and the army left.

❖

Sophia was walking down a street when a man rushed out of a store and the two collided with great force. The man was furious and cursed Sophia. Sophia made a little bow and said, "My friend, I do not know which of us is responsible for this encounter, but I am not inclined to investigate. If I ran into you, I beg your pardon, and if you ran into me, don't mention it."

Then Sophia smiled and walked away.

☙Lighten Up❧

Sophia was frustrated by the divisive nature of humanity. So, in order to try and make a difference in the world, she built a cage and inside the cage she put a dog and a cat. After a little training, she got the dog and the cat to the point where they could live peacefully together inside the same cage.

Then she added a pig, a goat and a kangaroo. With some training, they all lived together peacefully.

Then she added some birds and a monkey. With some training and a few adjustments, they all lived together in harmony.

She was so encouraged by those successes that she traveled the world and brought back an Irish Catholic, an American Presbyterian, a Hungarian Jew, a Turkish Muslim, a Japanese Buddhist.

In a very short time, there wasn't a single living thing left in the cage.

In a war of ideas it is people who are the casualties.
Anthony de Mello

Once, during a Sabbath service, a rabbi was seized by a sudden wave of guilt, prostrated himself and cried out, "God, before You I am nothing!"

The cantor was so moved by this demonstration of piety

that he threw himself to the floor beside the rabbi and cried, "God, before You I am nothing!"

Watching this scene unfold from his seat in the first row, the synagogue's janitor jumped up, flopped down in the aisle and cried, "God, before you I am nothing!"

The rabbi nudged the cantor and whispered, "So, look who thinks he's nothing!"

❖

Sophia's health was fading. Knowing her death was near she announced to all the monks that she soon would be passing down her robe to appoint the next teacher of the monastery. Her choice, she said, would be based on a contest. Anyone seeking the appointment was required to demonstrate spiritual wisdom by submitting a poem. The head monk, the most obvious successor, presented a poem that was well composed and insightful. All the monks anticipated his selection as their new leader.

However, the next morning another poem appeared on the wall in the hallway, apparently written during the dark hours of the night. It stunned everyone with its beauty and insight.

Determined to find this person, Sophia began questioning all the monks. The investigation led to the quiet kitchen worker.

Upon hearing the news, the jealous head monk and his comrades plotted to kill their rival.

In secret, Sophia passed down her robe to the kitchen worker, who quickly fled from the monastery, later to become a widely renowned wisdom teacher.

❖

People kill for money or for power. But the most ruthless murderers are those who kill for their ideas.

Anthony de Mello

❖

To a group of students who were arguing, Sophia told the following story, "One day a ferocious lion was stalking through the woods. He came to a giraffe. 'I'm King of the Jungle!' the lion screamed at the giraffe.

'Yipe!' yelped the giraffe as he ran through the jungle.

"The lion walked down to the river where he saw a crocodile floating in the water. 'I'm King of the Jungle!' the lion roared.

'Gulp!,' said the crocodile as he quickly swam away.

"Then the lion came upon a large bull in a field. 'I'm King of the Jungle!' he shouted. The bull didn't move. 'I'm King of the Jungle!' the lion roared even louder. Soon there was a ferocious battle between the lion and the bull. The lion defeated the bull and had him for lunch. Proud of himself, the lion roared, 'I'm King of the Jungle!' over and over again louder than he ever had before.

"Nearby, a hunter heard the lion and followed his boasts. He quickly captured the lion and carried him away to the circus.

"The moral of the story," Sophia said, "is that when you are full of bull, you are better off if you just keep your mouth shut."

❖

Listen or thy tongue will keep thee deaf.
                    American Indian Proverb

❖

A woman came hobbling down the street. "Poor Mary," said Sophia. "She has suffered for what she believes."

"And what does she believe?" asked a friend.

"She believes that she can wear a size six shoe on her size nine foot."

❖

"Don't spend so much time worrying about what other people think of you," Sophia instructed her students.

Their looks told Sophia they were unaware of what she was speaking about so she told them the story of the flea family and the elephant.

"Once a flea approached an elephant, 'Mr. Elephant, my family and I would like to move into your ear. We intend to be no trouble, would you mind if we live in your ear?' The elephant said nothing because he heard nothing. The flea added, 'If we are too rambunctious or too loud, just let us know.' Again the elephant said nothing.

"The flea family lived in the ear for a while. 'I don't like it here,' Mrs. Flea said. 'Let's move out.' Mr. Flea was concerned that the elephant would miss them when they left but consented to his wife's wishes. 'Mr. Elephant,' the flea said. 'I hate to tell you this. We are going to move. My wife wants a place more stationary. I'm sorry we'll have to leave, but you have been a marvelous host.' Again the elephant said nothing because he heard nothing or noticed nothing."

Her students still gave Sophia a puzzled look. "People don't think about you as much as you think they think of you." Her students nodded in understanding.

❖

Sophia was asked how she seemed so impervious to what people thought of her.

Sophia replied, "Before I was twenty, I wondered what people thought of me. After I was twenty, I worried about what others thought of me. Then one day, after fifty, I saw that people hardly thought of me at all."

❖

"Are there ways to gauge one's spiritual strength?" the student asked Sophia.

"Many," she replied.

"Tell me one,"

"Find out how often you become disturbed in the course of a single day," Sophia advised.

❖

I will not let anyone walk through my mind with their dirty feet.
Mohandas K. Gandhi

Sophia instructed a student to give money to everyone who insulted her for three years. After the three year term was over, she walked into a restaurant where a man was insulting everyone who came in the door.

"Why are you laughing while I insult you?" the man asked.

She replied, "To think I used to pay for this stuff when now I get it for free!"

A student came to Sophia and said, "I want to learn how to believe in God. I am a hard working and devoted student, how long will it take me to learn."

Sophia replied casually, "Ten years."

Impatiently, the student responded, "But I want to learn faster than that. I will work very hard. I will practice everyday, ten or more hours a day if I have to. How long will it take then?"

"Hmmm," said Sophia, "twenty years."

Most people with their beliefs are like an archer who shot his arrows first and then drew circles around where they landed.

Anthony de Mello

Sophia visited a monk who was depressed and angry.

"Why are you so frustrated?" she asked.

"Look at me," he said. "I've been here for 38 years and I have not yet attained pure prayer."

Sophia laughed. "I see what's so sad," she said. "It is that you can be here for 38 years and still think there is such a thing as pure prayer."

The preacher said, "The good news is that God is love, and God loves us if we obey God's commandments."

"*If?*" Sophia commented, "then the news isn't all that good."

❖

Sophia went to a fancy event. One of the guests said, "Sophia, your dress is on backwards. Your hair looks like it has never seen a comb. Plus, your shoes don't match."

"I know," replied Sophia, "I didn't want to try and fool anyone. I came dressed as I am because I am a backwards, disheveled person, and I seldom match."

❖

The elders of two villages met to try and solve a boundary issue between the two communities. As the discussion got heated, an elder from one village stood up and started to yell.

"Remember rule number twenty-seven," Sophia reminded. The elder nodded his head and sat back down.

The negotiations continued, another elder stood up and shouted. "Remember rule number twenty-seven," Sophia reminded.

This elder also nodded his head and calmed down.

This happened on two more occasions.

During a break, the chief of the other village commented to Sophia, "That rule number twenty-seven is great. What is it?"

"Rule number twenty-seven is: 'Don't take yourself so seriously,'" Sophia told him.

"That's great," he said. "What are your other rules?"

"There are no other rules," Sophia replied.

☙Play☙

One day Sophia went to a banquet. As she was dressed rather shabbily, no one let her in. So she ran home, put on her best dress and coat and returned.

Immediately, the host came over, greeted her and ushered her to the head of an elaborate banquet table.

When the food was served, Sophia took the bowl of soup and poured it all over her coat, "Drink up, my coat," she said.

The host came over and asked Sophia what she was doing.

Sophia replied, "I am feeding my coat. It is obvious that my clothes are the real guest of honor today, not me!"

"Why is there no lock on the door to your house?" a man asked Sophia.

"Because I have nothing to steal," she replied.

"Then how do you keep out troublesome people?"

"I ignore them until they go away," she said.

"Does it work?" he asked.

Sophia put her hands over her ears, closed her eyes, and started humming. Offended, the man walked away.

"It does work," she yelled after he was some distance away.

"Let us toss a coin and see who is right," a man challenged Sophia.

"Certainly," said Sophia, "heads I win, tails you lose."

A neighbor, famous for making excuses, knocked on Sophia's door and asked to borrow a rope.

"I can't let you have my rope," she said, "I'm using it out behind my house to tie up the wind."

"No one uses a rope to tie up the wind," he said.

"I know," she replied, "but when you don't want to do something, one excuse is as good as any other." And with that, she closed the door.

At a gathering where Sophia was present, people were discussing the merits of youth. They had all agreed that a person's strength decreases as years go by.

Sophia disagreed. She said, "In my old age, I have the same strength as I had in the prime of my youth."

"That's impossible," the men replied.

"In my yard," explained Sophia, "there is a massive stone. In my youth I used to try and lift it. I never succeeded. Neither can I lift it now. I haven't changed a bit."

Someone asked Sophia if she believed in luck. "Certainly," she said, with a twinkle in her eye. "How else can one explain the success of people one does not like?"

An innkeeper came to see Sophia, "I run a very nice, comfortable inn, but no matter what we do, we can't seem to get people to come inside."

"What is the name of the inn?" Sophia asked.

"The Silver Star," he replied.

"Change the name of your inn if you want to increase your business," she instructed.

"Impossible!" said the innkeeper. "It has been The Silver Star for generations and is well known."

"It's well known as The Silver Star,"

"Yes," he said.

"How's that working for you?" she asked.

"Not very well," he said.

"Here is what you do," she said. "Name your inn The Five Bells and hang a row of six bells over the entrance."

"Six bells? What good would that do?"

"Give it a try and see," Sophia said.

The innkeeper did as she advised. Many travelers passing by the inn saw the mistake and came in to point it out to the management as if each was the only one to notice the mistake. Once inside, they were impressed by the cordiality of the service and stayed on, increasing the inn keeper's business.

❖

One day Sophia went to her neighbors and asked to borrow an earthen mug. She was given it. The next day, she returned it with a little mug inside.

"Why bring us two mugs when you borrowed one?" they asked.

"In the middle of the night, I heard a groan," replied

- 43 -

Sophia. "I went to see what it was and found your mug had given birth to a baby, so I'm only returning what is yours."

The astonished neighbors said nothing and took the two mugs.

The next day, Sophia asked for the loan of a tin plate. She returned two plates and again told her neighbors that the bigger one had given birth. Delighted, they took both.

The next day, she came to borrow a glass pitcher and then returned the following day with two pitchers.

A week later, Sophia came and asked to borrow their silver lamp, and they readily gave it to her. When several days passed without any sign of her, they knocked on her door and said, "Neighbor, why haven't you returned the silver lamp we lent you?"

"I'm terribly sorry," replied Sophia, "but in the middle of the night I heard a groan. When I went to see what it was, I found your lamp had passed away."

"What?" said the neighbors dumbfounded. "How can a lamp die?"

"If a cup, a plate, and a pitcher can give birth," replied Sophia, "what's to keep a lamp from dying?"

The cupbearer to the king was frightened because he had broken the king's favorite cup. Afraid the king would have him killed for breaking the cup, the bearer went to Sophia for advice on how to tell him. He did as she instructed.

He went to the king with a sad look on his face.

"Why are you so sad, Cupbearer?"

"King, I am greatly disturbed about death," he said. "Why is there death?"

The king replied, "Do not be disturbed, death is part of

life, everything dies in its time. It is part of nature. Does that help you feel better?"

"Yes," said the servant handing him the broken pieces. "It was time for your cup to die."

Sophia's students asked about her boyfriend, "What does he like about you."

Sophia replied, "He thinks I'm talented, clever, beautiful, and a marvelous dancer."

"And what do you like about him?" they asked.

"I like that he thinks I'm talented, clever, beautiful, and a marvelous dancer," she replied.

❖

Sophia, walking late one night in a strange village tumbled into the community cesspool. No matter how hard she tried, she could not climb out, so she yelled, "Fire! Fire! Fire!"

Many from the town came running, and upon finding her, helped her out.

"Sophia," they asked, "why did you yell, 'Fire! Fire! Fire!?'"

"Well, would you have come if I yelled, 'Poop?'"

❖

Once, a renowned philosopher and moralist traveling through Sophia's village asked her to join him for dinner. They went to a nearby restaurant known for fresh fish.

The waiter brought out a large platter with two cooked fish, one quite a bit smaller than the other. Without hesitating, Sophia took the larger of the fish and put in on her plate.

The scholar gave Sophia a look of shock and disbelief. "What you just did was terribly selfish and was in violation of ethics and etiquette," he scolded.

Sophia listened to the philosopher's lecture patiently, and when he had finally finished said, "Well, Sir, what would you have done?"

"I, being a conscientious human, would have taken the smaller fish for myself," said the scholar.

"And here you are," Sophia said giving him the smaller fish.

A politician, famous for spinning the truth, finished giving his speech in the village and asked if there were any questions.

Sophia called out, "That donkey over there in the field, how many legs does it have?"

Frustrated by the question, but knowing that Sophia carried great respect in the village, he answered, "Four."

"What if you call the tail a leg, then how many legs would he have?" Sophia asked.

"Five," answered the politician.

"No," said Sophia, it doesn't matter what you call it. The tail is still a tail." And with that, she walked away.

Connect

A visitor spoke with Sophia, "I have walked through this town and am amazed at how many different churches there are. People here sure must love God."

"Yes," said Sophia, "they love God very much. It's each other they can't stand."

❖

One afternoon, Sophia and her friend were sitting in a cafe, drinking tea, and talking about life and love. "How come you never got married, Sophia?" asked her friend.

"Well," said Sophia, "to tell you the truth, I spent my youth looking for the perfect man. In Cairo, I met a beautiful and intelligent man with eyes like dark olives, but he was unkind. Then in Baghdad, I met a man who was a wonderful and generous soul, but we had no common interests. One man after another would seem just right, but there would always be something missing. Then one day, I met him. He was beautiful, intelligent, generous and kind. We had everything in common. In fact he was perfect."

"So," said Sophia's friend, "what happened? Why didn't you marry him?"

Sophia sipped her tea reflectively. "Well," she replied, "it's a sad thing, seems he was looking for the perfect woman."

❖

A pair of good ears will drink dry a hundred tongues.

Benjamin Franklin

After thirty years of watching television every night, a husband said to his wife, "Let's do something different and exciting tonight."

"What?" she asked.

"Let's change chairs."

When a man whose marriage was in trouble sought her advice, Sophia said, "You must learn to listen to your wife."

The man took this advice to heart and returned after a month to say that he had learned to listen to every word his wife was saying.

Said Sophia with a smile, "Now go home and listen to every word she isn't saying."

While Sophia read from the sacred text, many students slept. One student stayed awake and took notes.

"Sophia," he said after she had finished, "did you see how many imbeciles disrespected the scriptures by sleeping while you were talking?"

"Dear one," she said, "I would rather you had slept through the reading than to have disrespected the Creator by judging God's children so harshly and labeling God's beloved creation 'imbeciles.'"

❖

A Samurai approached Sophia, "Wise teacher, is there really a paradise and a hell?"

"Are you a soldier?" Sophia asked.

"Yes," the Samurai said proudly.

"What kind of ruler would have you as a soldier? You would disgrace any king for you have the face of a monkey!"

The Samurai drew his sword.

"Will you strike me with that dull stick? I'll bet you are barely strong enough to lift it."

He raised it back and started to yell. Just before he swung at Sophia's neck, she said, "This is the gate to hell."

Realizing the lesson he had just been given, in respect, he put his sword at Sophia's feet and bowed his head.

"And this," said Sophia, "is the gate to heaven."

❖

"How shall I forgive others?" the student asked.

"If you never condemned, you would never need to forgive," replied Sophia.

❖

Judgment and love are opposites. From one comes all the sorrows of the world. But from the other comes the peace of God.

A Course in Miracles

Sophia was teaching at a monastery.

One of the residents was caught stealing. The monks informed Sophia. She did nothing.

The same monk was caught stealing again.

Again Sophia was told and again she did nothing.

After the third transgression, several monks passed a petition that the thief be made to leave the monastery. The students who signed the petition threatened to leave if the thief was not cast out.

"We will miss you," Sophia said to the students who signed the petition. "But, I, in good conscience, cannot cast out one who needs my instruction so badly. Who needs to learn more than one who has not found a better way than stealing? He is a prime student. Even if you all leave, I will not cast out my prime student."

With her words, the monk who had stolen wept, and he never stole again.

Sophia went to the door of her beloved and knocked.

"Who is it?" the beloved asked.

"It is I," Sophia replied.

"This cottage is small. There is no room for the both of us."

Sophia went away.

She returned and knocked again.

"Who is it?" the beloved asked.

"It is you," Sophia replied.

The beloved let her in.

A shepherd was grazing his sheep when a passerby said, "That's a fine flock of sheep you have. Could I ask you something about them?"

"Of course," said the shepherd.

"How much would you say your sheep walk each day?"

"Which ones, the white ones or the black ones?"

"The white ones."

"Well, the white ones walk about four miles a day."

"And the black ones?"

"The black ones too."

"And how much wool would you say they give each year?"

"Which ones, the white or the black?"

"The white ones."

"Well, I'd say the white ones give some six pounds."

"And the black ones?"

"The black ones too."

The passerby was intrigued. "May I ask you why you have this strange habit of dividing your sheep into white and black each time you answer one of my questions?"

"Well," said the shepherd, "that's only natural. The white ones are mine, you see."

"Ah! And the black ones?"

"The black ones are mine, too," said the shepherd.

A couple of soldiers in northern India were riding in a rickshaw when they saw another with a couple of sailors in it. They challenged them to race. The sailors pulled ahead and were yelling victory until they saw the soldiers blow past them. They had gotten out of their rickshaw and were helping pull.

There were four towns. In each town, people were starving to death. Each town had a bag of seeds.

In the first town, no one knew what seeds could do. No one knew how to plant them. Everyone starved.

In the second town, one person knew what seeds were and how to plant them, but did nothing about it for one reason or another. Everyone starved.

In the third town, one person knew what seeds were and how to plant them. He proposed to plant them in exchange for being declared the king or ruler. All ate, but were ruled.

In the fourth town, one person knew what seeds were and how to plant them. He not only planted the seeds, but taught everyone the art of gardening. All ate, all were free, and all were empowered.

❖

Sophia asked her students, "A farmer who had the best corn at the county fair shared his seed with his neighbors. Why?"

The students did not know. "If he shares his seed, his corn will suffer. It will no longer be special," said one student.

"You are mistaken," replied Sophia. "His corn will actually get better. Do you know why?"

They did not.

"The wind picks up the pollen from his neighbors' fields and carries it to his farm. For him to keep having the best corn it would have to be pollinated by the best corn. By giving his seed away, his farm improved. As your neighbor lives so you live. Go and learn the lesson of the farmer."

"My life needs meaning," a student told Sophia.

Sophia took him into the forest and showed him a tiger lying upon the ground. The student was afraid of the tiger at first until he saw it was terribly wounded.

"How does it survive?" asked the student.

"Watch," encouraged Sophia.

After a couple of hours, they saw a fox bringing the tiger food.

"What did you learn?" she asked.

"God will provide," the student replied.

Some days later, walking in the forest, Sophia came upon the student lying upon the ground. "Silly child," she said. "I showed you the fox and tiger in the forest so you could learn to imitate the fox, not the tiger."

A minister came up to Sophia, knowing that she gave more questions than answers, he asked, "Sophia, I'm here on a retreat for spiritual growth. Would you give me a question?"

Sophia looked at him, thought for a moment, and said, "What do they need?"

The minister looked disappointed. "I'm sorry I wasn't clear," he said. "I'm not thinking about my congregation but myself. I am looking for a question that will help my own growth closer to God."

"Oh," said Sophia. She thought for another moment and said, "What do they really need?"

ଓଃLet Goଃ

Sophia came to the front door of the king's palace. She entered and made her way to where the king himself was sitting on his throne.

"What do you want?" asked the king, immediately recognizing Sophia.

"I would like a place to sleep in this inn," replied Sophia.

"But this is not an inn," said the king, "it is my palace."

"May I ask who owned this palace before you?"

"My father. He is dead."

"And who owned it before him?"

"My grandfather. He too is dead."

"In this place people live for a short time and then move on. Did I hear you say that it is not an inn?"

A man came to Sophia, "Sophia, your wisdom is known far and wide, can you help me find a way to make more money?"

"Do you know the purpose of a window?" she asked.

"To see the world," he replied.

"Do you know what happens when you cover a window with silver?"

The man thought for a moment and replied, "It becomes a mirror."

"So too in your life, cover it with silver and you stop seeing the world and only see yourself. Be careful."

❖

Once upon a time there was a man touring Africa. In a remote area he saw a beautiful set of birds in the trees. He threw a net over one and took it home. He kept it in a large cage. Over time, the bird learned to speak.

The man was returning to Africa, before he left, he said to the bird, "I am returning to your native land. I will see some of your friends there. Is there anything you would like to tell them?"

"Yes," said the bird. "Tell them that although I am caged and can no longer fly free, I am very happy here. Tell them not to worry about me."

"I will," said the man.

He returned to Africa and found the trees where he had caught the exotic bird. There he told the other birds, "I have your friend in my home. He said to tell you, 'Although I am caged and can no longer fly free, I am very happy here. Tell them not to worry about me.'" When the man finished speaking, one of the birds in the tree fell down from the tree, dead. The man was startled.

He returned to his home. He told his bird, "I saw your friends, a very strange thing happened. When I told them that you were happy here in my home, one fell out of a tree, dead."

With that his bird fell over, dead.

Saddened at the loss of his exotic bird, and very puzzled, he took the body out of the cage and threw it on a trash heap in the back of his house. As soon as the body hit the trash heap, the bird came to life and flew up into a tree out of reach of the man.

"How can this be?" the man asked.

"My friend in Africa sent me a message. By falling to the ground dead, he told me that the only way I could be free was to die."

Sophia awoke one night to a burglar in her house.

She helped him to as much as he could carry. She opened the door for him on his way out.

She walked outside and looked up in the clear night sky.

"What I really wish I could have given him was this moon," she said.

"What did enlightenment bring you?" the student asked.

"Joy," Sophia replied.

"And what is joy?"

"The realization that when everything is lost you have only lost a toy."

"Problems and challenges can bring growth and enlightenment," said Sophia. Then she explained, "Each day, a bird would shelter in the withered branches of a tree that stood in the middle of a vast deserted plain. One day, a whirlwind uprooted the tree, forcing the poor bird to fly a hundred miles in search of shelter until it finally came to a forest of fruit-laden trees. If the withered tree had survived, nothing would have induced the bird to give up its security and fly."

A traveler came to see Sophia after hearing about her teachings. He was surprised to see Sophia lived in a small home with only a few books, a table and a few chairs.

"Sophia," the visitor asked, "where are your belongings? Where is your furniture?"

"Where is yours?" Sophia asked.

"Mine? I'm just a traveler here. I am just passing through."

"Me, too," Sophia replied.

When the sparrow builds its nest in the forest, it occupies but a single branch. When the deer drinks from the river, it takes no more than its belly can hold. We collect things because our hearts are empty.

Unknown

Sophia sat in meditation on the riverbank when a student bent down to place two enormous pearls at her feet as a gift.

She opened her eyes to see the pearls. She picked one up, but dropped it. It rolled down the hill and into the river. The student chased after it and looked all afternoon, diving, coming up for air, and diving back down.

"Sophia," he asked. "Could you show me where it went in? I can't find it."

"Right there," she said throwing the other pearl in the river.

In the pursuit of learning, every day something is acquired. In the pursuit of The Way, every day something is dropped.

Lao Tzu

To a student who loved possessions, Sophia said, "Close your eyes and imagine that you and every other living being and every possession has been thrown off a cliff. Each time you cling to someone or something to stop yourself from falling, just remember all of it is falling too."

❖

When they realized Sophia was going to die, her students wished to give her a worthy funeral. Sophia heard them and said, "Give me the sky and the earth for my coffin, the sun and moon and stars for my burial clothes, and all creation to escort me to the grave. Could I ask for anything more impressive?"

But her students wouldn't hear of it, protesting that she would be eaten by the animals and birds.

"Then make sure you place my staff near me that I might drive them away," Sophia said with a smile.

"How would you manage that? You will be unconscious."

"In which case it will not matter, will it, that I be devoured by the birds and beasts? Why should I care what happens to the wax when the candle is extinguished? Why should I care about the candle when the morning has come?"

☙Accept❧

There once was a man who had some problems. He went to Sophia for help. He said, "I like farming, but sometimes it doesn't rain enough, my crops fail, and we starve. Sometimes it rains too much, and my crops aren't what I want them to be."

Sophia did not say anything.

The man continued, "I'm married. She's a good wife. I love her, but sometimes she nags me. Sometimes I get tired of her."

Sophia did not say anything.

The man continued, "I have kids. Good kids, but sometimes they don't show me enough respect."

Sophia did not say anything. The man continued in several other areas of his life. He waited for Sophia to say something, but Sophia didn't say anything. "Well," said the man, "can you help me?"

Sophia said, "I can't help you. Everybody's got problems. In fact, we've all got eighty-three problems, and there's nothing you can do about it. If you work really hard on one of them, maybe you can fix it – but if you do another one will pop right into its place..."

The man became furious. "I thought you were wise!" he shouted. "I thought you could help me! What good are you if you can't help me?"

Sophia was quiet, then, after a moment, she replied, "Maybe I can help you. You are different from other people. Whereas everyone else has eighty-three problems, you have eighty-four problems. Most of your suffering comes from your eighty-fourth problem. I think I can help you with your eighty-fourth problem."

"You can?" the man asked. "What is my eighty-fourth problem?"

"Your extra problem is that you think you're not supposed to have any problems."

❖

"Sophia," a man cried, "life is so miserable in my home. Our little house is just too crowded. We just can't seem to get along anymore, lots of fussing and fighting. I just can't take it anymore."

"Do you have a goat?" Sophia asked.

"Yes."

"Take the goat into your home," Sophia instructed.

"What? Take the goat inside?"

"Yes," replied Sophia. "Trust me."

The disturbed father went back to his home and put his goat inside the house with his family. The next day, he returned to see Sophia.

"I did as you told me, but that goat just gets in the way. Now the house smells, and he's eating everything he comes near. My house is worse than ever. What should I do?"

"Do you have any chickens?" asked Sophia.

"Of course."

"Then take them into your home."

"What? The chickens too?" asked the man.

"Yes," replied Sophia. "Trust me."

So the man went home and brought all his chickens inside his house. The next day, he came back.

"Sophia, I am going insane. As if the smell isn't bad enough, all that continuous clucking is about to drive me crazy. We are so overcrowded. What am I going to do?"

"Very well," said Sophia, "go home and take the goat out."

The next day, he returned and said, "Sophia, it's a little better, but still all that clucking."

Sophia nodded, "Throw out the chickens."

The next day, the man came back with a big smile on his face. "Sophia, there is no one in the whole world as wise as you. My house is a paradise!"

A man came to Sophia, huffing after his third attempt to climb the mountain near her village.

"Sophia," he said. "I can't understand it. I trained so hard before I came to your village to climb the mountain. Yet, half way up, I get so tired and winded while even the smallest woman from your village carrying a large bundle on her head passes me by. How can this be?"

"It's simple," said Sophia. "You are trying to conquer the mountain. You see the mountain as your opposition. The people of my village love the mountain. They see it as their friend. So, while you are battling the mountain up the hills, my people are simply strolling with a companion."

A king asked Sophia for a blessing.

Sophia said, "May you die. May your son die. Then may your son's son die."

The king was furious, "What kind of blessing is this, wishing that me, my son and my grandson die?"

"It is a wonderful blessing," stated Sophia. "How horrible a tragedy when children die before their parents. What I wished for you is the perfect order of life."

❖

Sophia went to see a member of her village after a fire burned her house to the ground. "This should make dying easier," she offered.

❖

When it became clear that Sophia would die, her students were sad.

"Don't you see that death gives loveliness to life?" Sophia said.

"We'd rather you never die," the students replied.

"Don't you see that whatever is truly alive dies? Only plastic flowers never die."

❖

Sophia was walking along one day when a tiger started to chase her. Running from the tiger, she hurried along the edge of a cliff and fell over. Part way down, she grabbed a vine stopping her fall.

She looked above and saw the tiger looking over the edge at her. She looked below, and there was another tiger at the bottom.

The vine she was holding onto started to pull from the side of the cliff.

She noticed a strawberry growing on the vine. She pulled it and ate. It tasted very sweet.

❖

"What is the secret of your serenity?" a student asked Sophia

"Wholehearted cooperation with the inevitable," she replied.

❖

Sophia lived with a family on a small farm. They were not rich. They had simply a small barn and a good horse they used to plow the fields and ride to town when the occasion arose.

One day, the horse ran away. The farmer said, "Oh no! I lost my horse. That's bad."

Sophia replied, "Maybe. I don't know if it is good or bad. Only God can say."

A week later, the horse returned, but it wasn't alone. The horse brought home a wild stallion companion. Both horses were placed in the corral. The farmer said, "Wow, we have two horses. That's good!"

Sophia replied, "Maybe. I don't know if it is good or bad. Only God can say."

A few days later, the farmer's son was trying to tame the new horse. The stallion threw the son off its back. When the son hit the ground he broke his hip. Though he healed, he never was quite the same and walked with a limp. The farmer moaned, "Oh, my son broke his hip, that's bad."

Sophia replied, "Maybe. I don't know if it is good or bad. Only God can say."

A year later, the army came through the nearby village. The army was short on troops, so they took every young and able man of the village and surrounding area with them. When they came by the farm, they did not take the farmer's son since he still traveled slowly with his limp. The farmer said to Sophia, "The army didn't take my son. Isn't that good?"

Sophia replied, "Maybe. Only God can say." She paused for a moment and whispered, "But I think it's pretty good."

❖

Sophia slipped into the rapids of a river in front of a high and dangerous waterfall. A man on the shore watched in horror. Fearing for Sophia, the spectator ran down the path along the river and climbed down the side of the waterfall. He expected to see her body floating in the water. Instead he saw Sophia walking to the shore, unharmed, wringing the water from her hair.

"How did you do it?" he asked. "How could you survive such a terrible fall?"

"Simple," Sophia responded. "I just went with the flow. I became one with the water, so as the water plunged, I plunged. As the water swirled, I swirled. As the water came out, I came out."

ଓOpenଔ

Sophia encountered a man always in a hurry.

"Why are you rushing so?" Sophia asked.

"I am chasing after God," he replied. "I want to know more, see more, and do more. In pursuit of God, there is no time to waste."

"How do you know," Sophia asked, "that God is out in front of you for you to run after? God may be pursuing you. To encounter God, all you need to do is stand still, but instead you keep running away."

Sophia, rummaging through the library, pulled out a book and claimed, "I have just found a book that tells us everything we can conceivably know about God."

The students gathered around, though they had spent a lot of time in the library, they did not recognize the book.

Sophia put the book on a table and opened it, turning through it page by page. Every page was blank.

"But the book says nothing," wailed the librarian.

"Yes," said Sophia, "but see how much it indicates."

The free person is the one who does not fear to go to the end of his thought.

Leon Blum

Sophia came back from the desert and her time of prayer.

"Tell us what God is like," her students demanded.

She didn't know how to describe the indescribable, so she offered a principle, a statute, a formula, in hopes that some of them might be encouraged to go into the desert of their lives, and open their hearts to God.

But they seized upon the formula, made it a text, spread it to foreign lands, imposed it on others as a holy belief.

Sophia wondered if it would have been better if she had said nothing at all.

"Most every word and image we use to speak about God is more a distortion than a description," Sophia said.

"Then how do we speak of God?" the students asked.

"Through silence," Sophia replied.

"Why then do you speak about God in words?" they asked.

Sophia laughed, "When I speak, don't listen to the words. Hear the silence."

❖

It is impossible for a person to learn when he thinks he already knows.

Epictetus

❖

Her students were amazed that Sophia never seemed to be baited by the scholars to their endless debates about the nature of God. She replied, "Why talk about the ocean to a frog in a well, or about the divine to people limited by their concepts."

❖

Concepts create idols; only wonder comprehends anything. People kill one another over idols. Wonder makes us fall to our knees.
                                        Saint Gregory of Nyssa

❖

"I wish to follow God," the student told Sophia.
"Are you willing to give up your possessions?"
"Yes," replied the student.
"Your dreams?"
"Yes."
"Loved ones?"
"Yes."
"Your life?"
"Yes."
"There is then only one thing left to give up to truly follow God?" said Sophia.
"What is it?" asked the student. "I am ready."
"You must give up your ideas and beliefs about God."
The student walked away sadly because he held tightly to his convictions, he feared ignorance more than death.

"Is there a God?" asked the professor.

"Certainly not the kind people are thinking of," said Sophia.

"Whom are you referring to when you speak of people?"

"Everyone," she replied.

The eye sees only what the mind is prepared to comprehend.
Henri L. Bergson

"Sophia, can you teach us to pray?" her students asked.

"Pray like the farmer, who lost his prayer book," she instructed. "After looking for it all day he gave up, and at night, he prayed, 'Creator, I lost my prayer book today. I don't know what to say. So, tonight I am just going to recite the alphabet over and over. You take the letters and arrange them as you choose.' Pray with an open heart like him."

"Sophia, what happens after death?" a student asked.

"How should I know?" she replied.

"Because you are a wise teacher."

"Yes," she said, "but not a dead wise teacher."

Sophia attacked the different notions about God that people entertained. "If your God comes to your rescue and gets you out of trouble, it is time you started searching for the true God."

When asked to elaborate, this is the story she told:

"A man left a brand-new bicycle unattended at the marketplace while he went about his shopping. He only remembered the bicycle the following day and rushed to the marketplace, expecting it would have been stolen. The bicycle was exactly where he had left it. Overwhelmed with joy, he rushed to a nearby temple to thank God for having kept his bicycle safe only to find, when he got out of the temple, the bicycle was gone."

A traveler was passing through town when he came upon a huge funeral procession. Sophia was on a corner watching the people pass by.

"Who died?" the traveler asked Sophia.

"I don't know," replied Sophia, "but I think it's the one in the coffin." Then she whispered, "These days, you never know for sure."

Belief as to faith is the difference between a baby bird sitting in the nest flapping its wings and another baby bird actually trying to fly.
Anthony de Mello

❖

While on a trip to another village, Sophia lost her favorite copy of Scriptures.

Several weeks later, a goat walked up to Sophia, carrying the Scriptures in its mouth.

Sophia was shocked. She took the precious book out of the goat's mouth, raised her eyes heavenward and exclaimed, "It's a miracle!"

"Not really," said the goat. "Your name is written inside the cover."

ᘓEmptyᘔ

Sophia was carrying a large sack thrown over her shoulder, her back bent from the weight.

A student approached, "Sophia, can I ask you a question?"

"Sure," she replied.

"Sophia, why do you pray?"

She stopped and set her bag down.

"I see," said the student. "And what is the result of your prayers?"

She picked her bag up and walked on down the street.

A samurai went to see Sophia. "I am a master of war. I want to learn to be a master of peace."

"You want to master peace?" Sophia asked the samurai.

"Yes," said the samurai.

"Great," said Sophia. "First, let's have a cup of tea."

The two knelt at the table. Sophia put out two cups. First, one to the samurai and then one to herself, then she started filling the samurai's cup. She poured until it overflowed, over the brim, across the table and then onto the samurai. All the while, Sophia hummed a tune.

The samurai felt insulted. He jumped up, drew his sword and raised it over his head to strike Sophia. Then she said, "You are not ready to learn the way of peace. You are not ready to learn at all. You are like this cup. You are so full of yourself that you have no room to learn anything. Empty yourself and then you will be prepared to learn."

It is not the answer that enlightens, but the question.

Decouvertes

Miriam went to Sophia to learn meditation.

Sophia told her to focus on this famous puzzle, "What is the sound of one hand clapping?"

Miriam went away and came back a week later shaking her head. She could not get it.

"Get out!" said Sophia. "You are not trying hard enough. You still think of this life. You would be closer to understanding if you died."

The next week Miriam came back again. When Sophia asked her, "What is the sound of one hand clapping?" she clutched at her heart, groaned and fell down as if dead.

"Well," said Sophia, "you have taken my advice and died, but what about the sound of one hand clapping?"

Miriam opened one eye, "I have not solved that yet."

"Dead women don't speak!" said Sophia, and she chased her out of the Temple.

It is not the notes but the space between them that makes the music. It is not the bars but the space between them that holds the tiger.

Unknown

"What do I need in order to be enlightened?" a student asked.

Sophia replied, "You must discover what it is that falls in the water and does not make a ripple; moves through the trees and does not make a sound; enters the field and does not stir a single blade of grass."

"What is this thing?" asked the student.

"It is not a thing at all," she said.

"So it is nothing?"

"You might say so."

"Then how are we to search for it?"

"Did I tell you to search for it? It can be found but never searched for. Seek and you will miss."

Sometimes there would be a rush of noisy visitors and the silence of the monastery would be shattered.

The clatter and chatter would upset the students, but not Sophia who seemed just as content with the noise as with the silence. To the protesting students, she said, "Silence is not the absence of sound, but the absence of self."

❖

The student came to Sophia, "I want to learn from you."

"What do you bring?" she asked.

"Nothing," he replied.

"Drop it immediately," she said.

"How can I drop it? It is nothing."

"Then carry it around with you," she said.

Stillness is your essential nature.

What is stillness? The inner space or awareness in which the words on this page are being perceived and become thoughts.

Without this awareness, there would be no perception, no thoughts, no world.

You are that awareness disguised as a person.

Eckhart Tolle

As Sophia grew old, the disciples begged her not to die.

"If I do not go, how will you ever see?"

"What is it we fail to see when you are with us?" they asked.

Sophia would not say.

When the moment of her death was near, they asked, "What is it we will see when you are gone?"

With a twinkle in her eye, she said, "All I did was sit on the riverbank handing out river water. After I'm gone, I trust you will notice the river."

Sophia entered a formal reception area and sat down at the foremost elegant chair.

The host approached and said, "Madam, those places are reserved for guests of honor."

"Oh, I am more than a mere guest," replied Sophia confidently.

"Oh, so are you a diplomat?"

"Far more than that!"

"Really? So you are a minister, perhaps?"

"No, bigger than that too."

"Oh! So you must be the Queen," said the host sarcastically.

"Higher than that!"

"What?! Are you higher than the Queen? Nobody is higher than the Queen in this village!"

"Now you have it. I am nobody!" said Sophia.

❖

It is a characteristic of creatures that they make something out of something, while it is a characteristic of God that he makes something out of nothing. Therefore, if God is to make anything in you or with you, you must first become nothing. Hence go into your own ground and work there, and the works that you work there will all be living.
Meister Eckhart

I've said before that every craftsman
searches for what's not there
to practice his craft.

A builder looks for the rotten hole
where the roof caved in. A water-carrier
picks the empty pot. A carpenter
stops at the house with no door.

Workers rush toward some hint
of emptiness, which they then
start to fill. Their hope, though,
is for emptiness, so don't think
you must avoid it. It contains
what you need!

Rumi

In order to arrive at what you do not know
  You must go by a way which is the way of ignorance.
In order to possess what you do not possess
  You must go by the way of dispossession.
In order to arrive at what you are not
  You must go through the way in which you are not.
And what you do not know is the only thing you know
And what you own is what you do not own
And where you are is where you are not.

T.S. Eliot